This MAMMOTH belongs to

____

____

____

Tony Bradman and Joanna Burroughes

Not Like That, Like This!

One day, Dad took Thomas for a walk.

They left the house,
walked down the road,
went past the shops,
and came to the park.
And there before them was a long line
of iron railings.

“You won’t put your head through those, will you, Tom?” laughed Dad.

“What, like this?” said Thomas.

“Not like that, like *this*,” said Dad.
Thomas tried to get Dad’s head out,
but it was stuck fast.

Along came one old lady.

"Not like that, like *this*," she said,
and tried to slide Dad's head out with butter.
But it was stuck fast.

Along came two men with their dogs.

“Not like that, like *this*,” they said,
and tried to bend the railings.
But Dad’s head was stuck fast.

Along came three park keepers.

“Not like that, like *this*,” they said,
and tried to pull Dad’s head out.
Heave ho! But it was stuck fast.

Along came four people jogging.

“Not like that, like *this*,” they said,
and tried something *very* different.
But Dad’s head was stuck as fast as ever.

Along came five boys on their bikes.

“Not like that, like *this*,” they said,
and tried to push Dad’s head out.
But it was stuck fast.

Along came six mothers with their babies.

“Not like that, like *this*,” they said, and tickled Dad. That didn’t help at all, and Dad’s head was still stuck fast.

Along came seven girls skipping.

"Not like that, like *this*," they said and tried
to get Dad out with their ropes.
But he was stuck fast, just the same.

Along came eight roller skaters.

"Not like that, like *this*," they said and tried their best. Dad liked the music, but his head was still stuck fast.

Along came nine policemen.

“Not like that, like *this*,” said the sergeant,
and took down all the details.
And Dad’s head was still stuck as fast as ever.

Then along came ten firemen
in a great big fire engine,

dang-a-lang-a-lang-a-lang.

“Not like *that*,” said the chief fireman,
“like THIS!” Dad was free at last,
and everybody cheered . . . hurray!
“How did it happen?” asked the chief fireman.

"I told Tom not to put his head through the railings," said Dad.
"What, like this?" said the fireman.
"Not like that," said Tom . . .

"like *this*!"

First published in Great Britain 1988
by Methuen
Published by Mammoth 1996
an imprint of Reed International Books Ltd
Michelin House, 81 Fulham Road, London SW3 6RB
and Auckland, Melbourne, Singapore and Toronto

ISBN 0 7497 2415 3

A CIP catalogue record for this title
is available from the British Library

Produced by Mandarin Offset Ltd
Printed and bound in Hong Kong